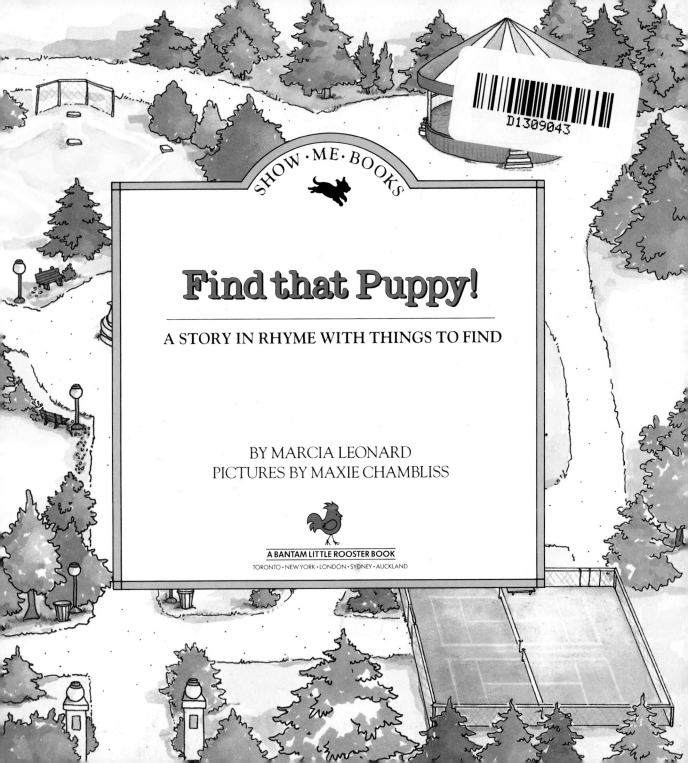

SHOW · ME · BOOKS

Find that Puppy!

A STORY IN RHYME WITH THINGS TO FIND

BY MARCIA LEONARD
PICTURES BY MAXIE CHAMBLISS

A BANTAM LITTLE ROOSTER BOOK
TORONTO · NEW YORK · LONDON · SYDNEY · AUCKLAND

In memory of my beloved mother,
who helped me write this book.
—M.L.

To Mike and Jessica
—M.C.

FIND THAT PUPPY!

A Bantam Book / November 1988

Produced by Small Packages, Inc.

"Bantam Little Rooster" is a trademark of Bantam Books.

All rights reserved.
Text copyright © 1988 by Small Packages, Inc.
Illustrations copyright © 1988 by Small Packages, Inc.,
and Maxie Chambliss.
No part of this book may be reproduced or transmitted
in any form or by any means, electronic or mechanical,
including photocopying, recording, or by any information
storage and retrieval system, without permission in
writing from the publisher.
For information address: Bantam Books.

Library of Congress Cataloging-in-Publication Data

Leonard, Marcia.
  Find that puppy!

  (Show me books)
  Summary: A rhyming text follows a puppy on a spree
through the park and asks readers to point out or
find various things in the illustrations.
  [1. Dogs—Fiction. 2. Parks—Fiction. 3. Literary
recreations. 4. Stories in rhyme] I. Chambliss,
Maxie, ill. II. Title. III. Series: Leonard, Marcia.
Show me books.
PZ8.3.L54925Fi 1988   [E]   88-3410
ISBN 0-553-05429-5

Published simultaneously in the United States and Canada

Bantam Books are published by Bantam Books, a division of Bantam
Doubleday Dell Publishing Group, Inc. Its trademark, consisting of the
words "Bantam Books" and the portrayal of a rooster, is Registered in U.S.
Patent and Trademark Office and in other countries. Marca Registrada.
Bantam Books, 666 Fifth Avenue, New York, New York 10103.

PRINTED IN THE UNITED STATES OF AMERICA

RM   0 9 8 7 6 5 4 3 2 1

This is the story of Annie and Joe,
who go to the park with their puppy named Bo.
The rhymes in this book will tell of their spree
and ask you about all the things that you see.

First the kids stop at a bench painted red.
They tell Bo to sit while they scatter some bread.
But Anne drops the leash to feed a big goose,
and Bo sees his chance—the next moment he's loose.

Catch that puppy!

Look at this picture and point out to me
a bluejay, a pigeon, a squirrel in a tree.
Then show me a chipmunk with stripes down his back,
some birds that say HONK! and some more that go QUACK!

What other animals do you see?

Bo sniffs the fall air. What is that good smell?
He follows the scent as if under a spell.
It leads to a picnic and food that looks great.
Anne and Joe chase him—but they are too late.

Where's that puppy?

Look at this picture for good things to eat,
for something that's sour and something that's sweet.
Find apples and grapes, find hot dogs and steak,
tomatoes, potato chips, carrots, and cake.

What else can you find?

Bo hears a nice sound. He runs toward the noise and soon finds himself among small girls and boys. Joe and Anne trail him, they search high and low, but Bo can't be found. Where did that dog go?

That naughty puppy!

Look at this picture. Can you find the pup?
A boy sliding down and a girl climbing up?
Do you see a baby who's lost a pink shoe?
A girl who jumps over, a boy who crawls through?

What else are the children doing?

Bo's getting tired; it's time for a nap.
He sees a big lady and jumps in her lap.
Annie and Joe stop to rest quite nearby,
but they don't see Bo. Can you tell me why?

Oh, that puppy!

Look at this picture and find wheels galore:
a bike with two wheels and a stroller with four.
Find wheels on a cart and wheels on a truck;
then look for some wheels on a small yellow duck.

What other wheels do you see?

Bo's had his rest, now he's ready to go.
He jumps from his perch and runs past Anne and Joe.
They dash after him and come to a stand,
where someone is singing along with a band.

Now where's that Bo?

Look at this picture and point to the drums;
then show me the banjo a country boy strums.
Can you find a fiddler who plays with a bow?
A girl with a mouth harp who's tapping her toe?

What else can you show me?

The band takes a break. The kids spot their pet!
But he runs away and gets caught in a net.
The game has to stop; the players all glare.
Anne and Joe pounce—but they miss by a hair!

Get that puppy!

Look at this picture and count sets of four:
four rackets, four tennis balls. Do you see more?
Four players, four visors that shade from the sun.
Can you count more fours, or is your counting done?

What else can you count?

Joey and Anne are fed up with their dog.
They give up the chase and sit down on a log.
But look who appears from his last hiding place!
It's Bo with a "Here I am!" look on his face.

That silly old puppy.

Look at this picture, look close to the ground.
Can you see where toadstools and flowers are found?
Find soft curly ferns and prickly pine cones,
some bright colored leaves and some moss-covered stones.

What other small things do you see?

All is forgiven—the kids love their Bo!
Joe picks up the leash and they're ready to go.
They've had a fine time. The chase was great fun!
Good-bye to the park and good-bye to the sun.